This **Monkey & Cake** book
belongs to:

YOUR Mom

For Dorothy –D.D.

My technique is a mix of dark pencils and acrylic. I use watercolor brushes with marten hairs and paper with no grain, usually Sennelier or Arches 300g. For my characters, I spend time observing attitudes and how children move, talk, and dance.

–Olivier Tallec

Text copyright © 2019 by Drew Daywalt
Illustrations copyright © 2019 by Olivier Tallec

Library of Congress Cataloging-in-Publication Data available
ISBN 978-1-338-14386-7

10 9 8 7 6 5 4 3 2 1 • 19 20 21 22 23
Printed in China   62
First edition, April 2019
The text type and display type was set in Burbank. • Book design by Jess Tice-Gilbert

a **Monkey & Cake** book

What Is Inside THIS Box?

Written by **Drew Daywalt** • Illustrated by **Olivier Tallec**

Orchard Books
New York
An Imprint of Scholastic Inc.

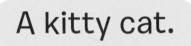

A
kitty cat
is inside
the box?

Ooh!
I love kitty cats.
Can I see it?

No, you cannot.
It is a magic cat.

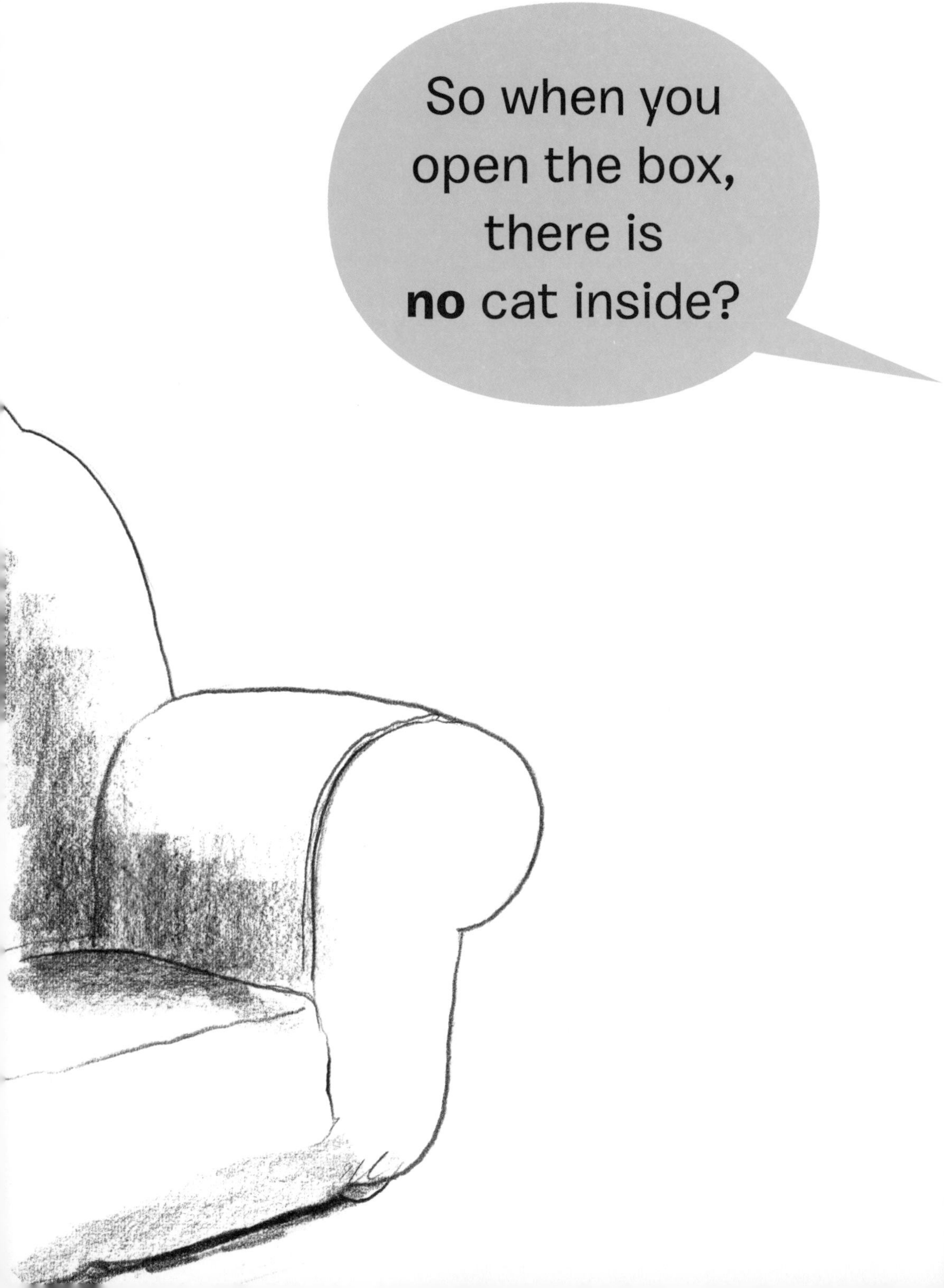
So when you open the box, there is **no** cat inside?

How do
you know
there
IS NOT
a cat
in the box
when
it is closed?

Then I think
there is a dinosaur
in the box
when it is closed.

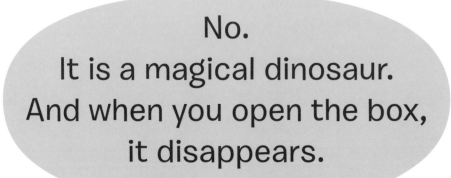

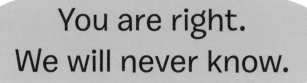

THE END